BASKETBALL

Junior Sports

Morgan Hughes

Rourke
Publishing LLC
Vero Beach, Florida 32964

www.rourkepublishing.com

PHOTO CREDITS: Cover Anton Want/Getty; p 5, 18 Stephen Dunn/Getty; p 6, 26, 28, 29 Photos.com; p 9 Elsa/Getty; p 11 David Rubinger/Getty; p 12 Brian Bahr/Getty; p 13 Aris Messinis/Getty; title page, p 15 Doug Pensinger/Getty; p 16 Isma'il Muhaammad/Getty; p 19 Darren McNamara/Getty; p 20 Ilmars Znotins/Getty; p 22 Chris Paul/Getty; p 23 Tatiana Makeyeva/Getty; p 25 Shelly Katz/Getty

ISBN 1-59515-189-3

Title page: *In addition to excellent physical conditioning, basketball requires top-notch hand-eye coordination for shooting, dribbling, and passing.*

Editor: Frank Sloan

Library of Congress Cataloging-in-Publication Data

Hughes, Morgan, 1957-
 Basketball / Morgan Hughes.
    p. cm. -- (Junior sports)
 Includes bibliographical references and index.
 ISBN 1-59515-189-3 (hardcover)
 1. Basketball--Juvenile literature. I. Title. II. Hughes, Morgan, 1957-
Junior sports.
 GV885.1.H84 2004
 796.323--dc22
                                          2004009369

Printed in the USA

CG/CG

TABLE OF CONTENTS

HOOP BASICS

In 1891, a teacher named Dr. James Naismith **invented** basketball. He wanted a game to keep college athletes in shape during winter months in New England. Today basketball is a favorite sport for boys and girls of all ages, and the Basketball Hall of Fame in Springfield, Massachusetts, is named after Naismith's invention.

Basketball is a fast-paced game with lots of running, positioning, and shooting.

Basketball can be played just as easily indoors on a hardwood floor as outside in a school yard. You can even shoot balls in the driveway of your home. The standard basketball court is a **rectangle** roughly twice as long as it is wide. It usually measures about 92 feet (28 m) by 50 feet (15 m).

Baskets have two parts: a stiff circular metal rim about 18 inches (46 cm) in **diameter** and some form of nylon netting. Together, these hang from a backboard suspended 10 feet (3 m) above the floor at each end of the court. Shooting the ball through the basket is, of course, the object of the game.

While it helps to be tall, there have been some great NBA stars who were below average height even by standards of the everyday population.

The rectangular box painted on the backboard is a good target area for shooters.

THE PLAYERS

Basketball is played with a five-member team. Included are a center, usually the tallest, strongest player; two forwards, who are very good shooters; and two guards, who are quick and **agile**. The guards cover the opposition's forwards and begin offensive plays by moving the ball up-court.

In addition to good sneakers that support them, players in organized leagues wear uniforms consisting of lightweight nylon shorts and a sleeveless jersey designed for coolness and comfort.

Basketball players come in different sizes and shapes, but it's how they work together that means success or failure on the court.

SCORING SHOTS

Field goals are the most common scoring shots in basketball. They are taken from the field rather than from the foul line at the top of the 12-foot- (3.6 m-) long lane. Each field goal is worth two points. Field goals may be attempted from anywhere on the court.

The lay-up is the safest shot in the game, and the easiest for young players to master. It is taken from almost directly under the hoop, usually with one hand. The ball is bounced against the backboard just above the hoop, where it then **ricochets** back through the hoop for two points.

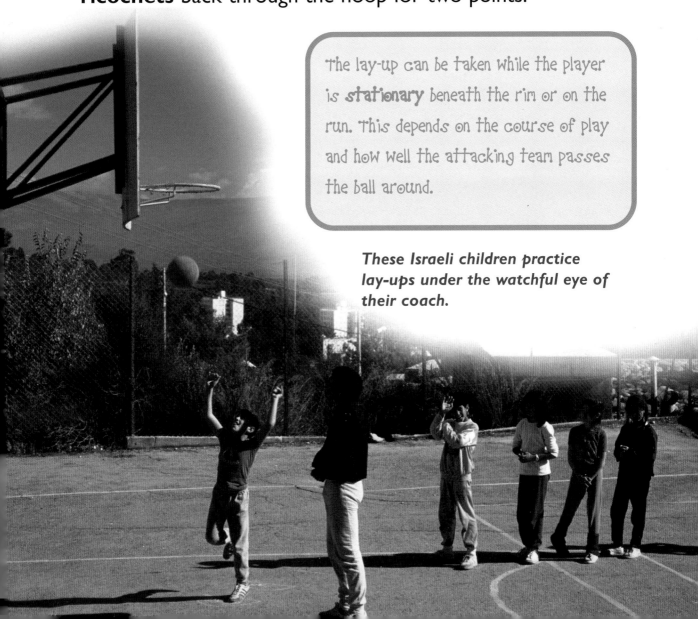

The lay-up can be taken while the player is **stationary** beneath the rim or on the run. This depends on the course of play and how well the attacking team passes the ball around.

These Israeli children practice lay-ups under the watchful eye of their coach.

Foul shots occur when the referee sees a **violation** of rules. For example, it is illegal to hit or slap the hand or arm of a player who's shooting the ball. In such a case, the offended player shoots from the foul line (or free throw line), while the other players line up along the outside of the lane.

Players lined up along the edge of the lane cannot go for the rebound until the shooter has made his free throw.

The hook shot can be very effective. When executed properly, the shooter is able to protect the ball by keeping it far from the reach of the defender. With good hand-eye coordination, the shooter can smoothly lob the ball toward the nearby hoop.

The hook shot is effective because the defender can't reach over to block it without risking a foul against the shooter.

DRIBBLING

The ball may only be advanced up and down the court in two ways: by passing it or by running with it. The second method must be accompanied by dribbling, or bouncing the ball as you run. Good ball control begins and ends with expert dribbling.

On the fast break, a player must combine dribbling, sprinting, and instinct.

All young basketball players must learn to dribble. They must know how to dribble while walking, jogging, and running. And they must dribble equally well with either hand. Only hours and hours of practice can achieve these basic skills. There are many drills at all levels to make this fun.

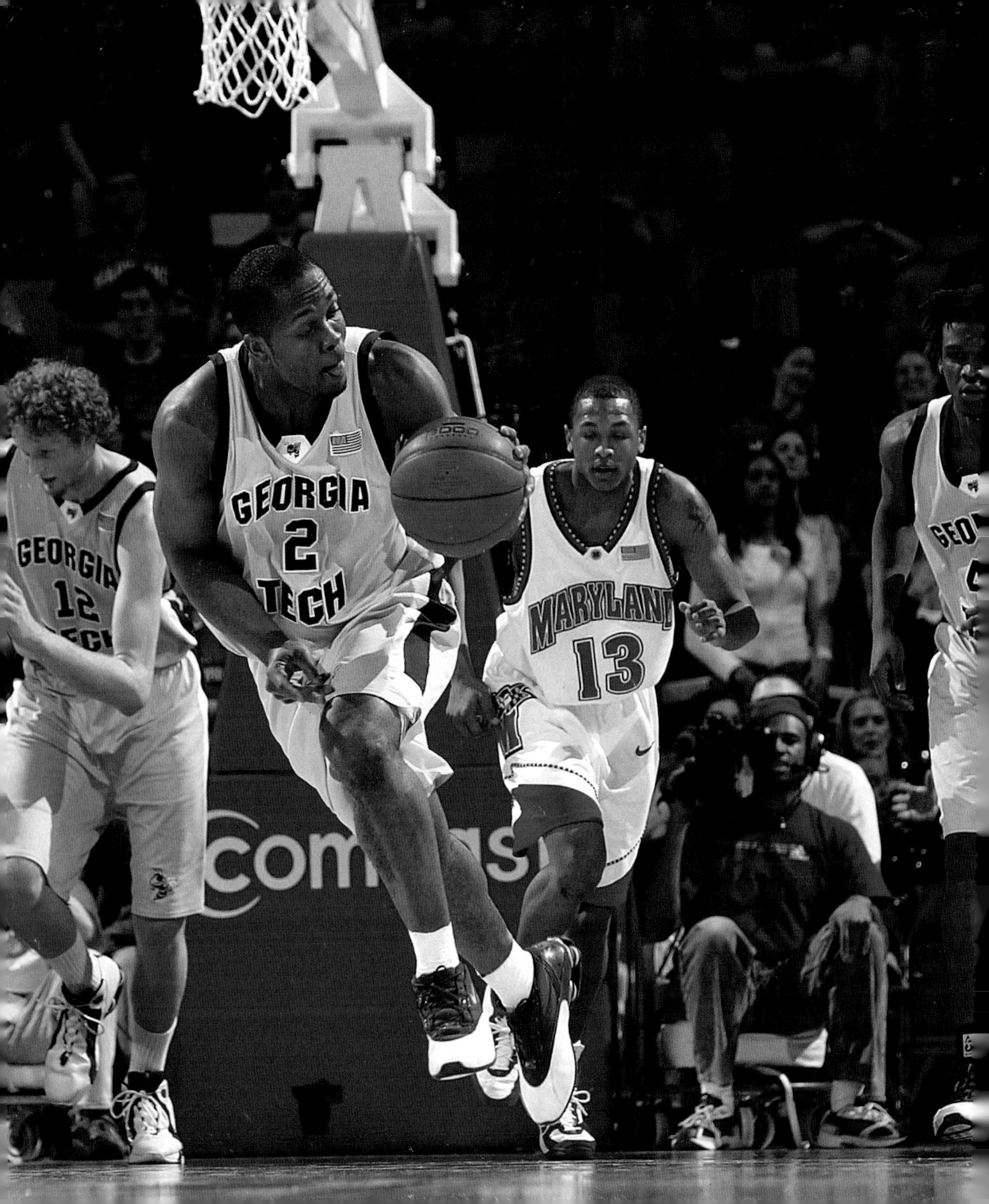
GEORGIA TECH 2
GEORGIA 12
MARYLAND 13
comcast

PASSING

Basketball is a run-and-gun, high-scoring game. In the NBA, individual superstars often get all the attention. But there's more to it than that. Basketball is a team game that needs the **coordinated** effort of five players working together. This is best demonstrated through a team's passing game.

John Stockton played 15 years in the NBA and was one of the game's greatest passing playmakers. He finished as the NBA's all-time leader in assists with 15,806.

On the fast break, a player must combine dribbling, sprinting, and instinct.

The two most basic passing techniques are the chest pass and the push pass. The chest pass begins with both hands on the ball—the ball against the chest. With a springing release of the arms, the player fires the ball to an intended teammate.

The chest pass, performed here by Rebecca Lobo, combines strength and accuracy.

The push pass looks like a cross between a baseball throw and a football throw. It is made with only one hand and gets the ball to a teammate who is not too far away. It is quicker to release and can be done with either hand from a central starting position.

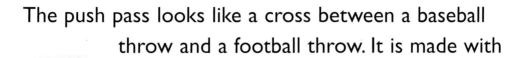

The push pass is a very popular technique players use to move the ball quickly around the court.

The bounce pass is a good choice when a defender has other outlets effectively blocked. It can be a one- or two-handed pass depending on positioning.

FOOTWORK

The fast pace and positioning of basketball requires correct stances and footwork. On defense, the key is to keep your feet moving, just wider than shoulder-width. Keep your knees comfortably bent. A defender must be able to shuffle quickly to keep up with an attacker running forward.

Playing defense is just as important as scoring points. With good footwork, you can stick to your opponent like glue.

Your hands are as important as your feet. While defending, they should be held out to the side to block passing lanes and to create a visual distraction. Also, by waving your arms, you might knock down a pass and produce a turnover.

Remember the name of the great playmaker who retired as the NBA's all-time assists leader? Well, that same John Stockton also finished with the most steals ever (3,265).

Hand position is a key to proper defensive play. Here former Olympic athlete Summer Sanders is ready to take the ball if the chance comes up.

You can make life very difficult for your opponent by blocking her view of the court.

REBOUNDING

Rebounding is the art of taking **possession** of the ball when a shot fails to go through the hoop for a field goal. Once the ball bounces off the rim or the backboard, it is up for grabs. The stronger and quicker team will grab more rebounds and control the game.

Defensive rebounding relies on positioning and strength. The defender must stand between the basket and any opponents and hold his/her ground. Offensive rebounding sometimes comes down to excellent timing and outfoxing the defender who has established position.

Any rebounder must be able to anticipate which way the ball will bounce and use strength to get to it before the opposing team does.

Women have been playing basketball almost as long as men have. In the early days, their uniforms were very formal.

THE WOMEN'S GAME

Girls and women have made tremendous strides in basketball in the last hundred years. Every year, more and more female athletes enter the world of competitive basketball, from middle school, through high school, college, and even to the pros.

Ann Meyers became the first (and so far only) woman to get a tryout with an NBA team when she was signed to a training camp deal with the 1979 Indiana Pacers.

Once a sport for six players, women's basketball now fields—like the men—five players. The only visible difference between the two games is the size of the ball. Because women have somewhat smaller hands, they play with a slightly smaller ball. Otherwise, the games are virtually identical.

Basketball is now more popular than ever among girls and young women.

One of the great things about basketball is that you can play on an organized team or you can shoot hoops by yourself in your driveway.

GLOSSARY

agile (AJ el) — able to move in a quick and easy fashion

coordinated (ko ORD duh nayt ed) — worked together in a common effort

diameter (dye AM uh tur) — a straight line passing through the center of a circle

invented (in VENT ed) — created or produced as brand new

rectangle (REK tan gul) — a box, two of whose sides are longer than the other two

ricochets (RICK uh SHAYZ) — rebounds, usually off a flat surface

stationary (STAY shun airy) — not moving, fixed in place

possession (puh ZESH un) — ownership

violation (VI uh LAY shun) — the breaking of a law, or rule in a game

Further Reading

Brown, Bruce. *101 Youth Basketball Games and Drills*. Coaches Choice, 2002

Gaitley, Stephanie V. *Five-Star Girls' Basketball Drills, 2nd Edition*. Wish Publishing, 2003

Gutman, Bill, et.al. *The Complete Idiot's Guide to Coaching Youth Basketball*. Alpha Books, 2003

Websites to Visit

Basketball.com @ www.basketball.com/

Basketball Hall of Fame @ www.hoophall.com

The Basketball Highway @ www.bbhighway.com

The National Basketball Association @ www.nba.com

Index

About the Author

Morgan Hughes is the author of more than 50 books on hockey, track and field, bicycling, and many other subjects. He lives in Connecticut with his wife, daughter, and son.